SCAREDY CATS

For Chloe

Find out more about the Scaredy Cats at Shoo's fabulous website: www.shoo-rayner.co.uk

ORCHARD BOOKS
96 Leonard Street, London EC2A 4XD
Orchard Books Australia
32/45-51 Huntley Street, Alexandria, NSW 2015
First published in Great Britain in 2005
First paperback edition 2005

A CIP catalogue record for this book is available from the British Library.
ISBN 1 84362 446 X (hardback)
ISBN 1 84362 745 0 (paperback)
1 3 5 7 9 10 8 6 4 2 (hardback)
1 3 5 7 9 10 8 6 4 2 (paperback)
Printed in Great Britain

Doctor Catkyll and Mr Hyde

Shoo Rayner

ORCHARD BOOKS

The doctor opened the surgery door, letting Molly out into the cold, moon-bathed night.

Molly froze in terror as a menacing shape staggered up the steps.

In a strangled whisper a figure cried, "Help me, Doctor! I've cut myself!"

As the doctor helped her patient into the surgery, something spattered and splashed over Molly's paws...BLOOD!

Molly shivered. She ran as fast as she could to the secret circle and told her friends in the Secret Society of Scaredy Cats what had happened.

"We only get patients at night if they've had an accident," Molly explained. "The doctor will make him better."

"Doctors are wonderful," said Kipling, their leader, "until they need a doctor themselves."

Silence fell upon the secret circle. Kipling's eyes narrowed into slits. He was ready to tell a story. The story they had all come to hear.

"This is a story about my cousin, Candy," Kipling began. "She also lived with a doctor.

"Doctor Catkyll was wonderful – so kind and caring. Everybody loved him. Candy loved him most of all."

In the evenings, when the surgery was closed, Doctor Catkyll would go to his small laboratory where he carried out scientific experiments.

As the good doctor mixed up his lotions and potions, he told Candy what he was doing.

“I’m making medicines to help sick people,” he told her. “I have to mix these chemicals very carefully, otherwise the medicine might be poisonous!”

Candy didn't understand much about science. She just loved to be with the doctor and listen to his gentle voice.

Candy stayed with Doctor Catkyll through many long nights of hard work. His apparatus bubbled and gurgled, as medicines dripped into shiny glass bottles.

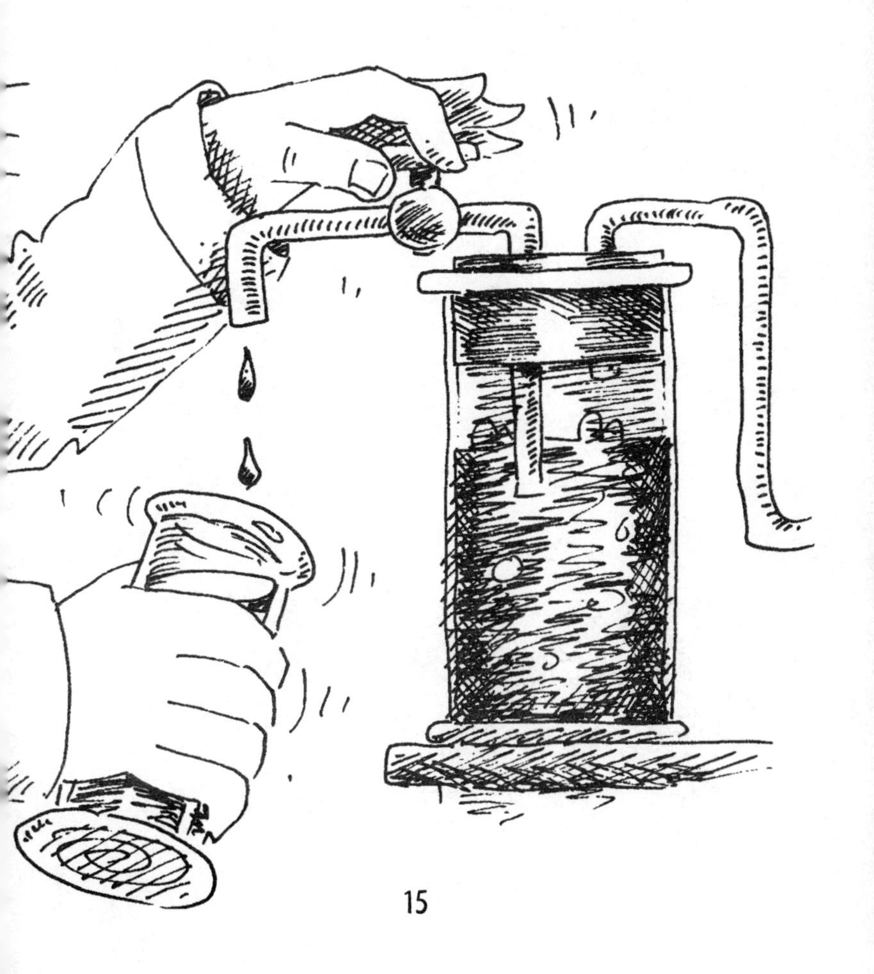

One night, Doctor Catkyll showed Candy a bottle of bright green liquid.

"If this medicine works it will cure the suffering of millions of sick people," he said lifting the bottle. "I shall have to test it myself."

The doctor startled Candy by throwing back his head and drinking the slimy-green contents of the bottle in one gulp.

Suddenly, the doctor groaned, clutched his stomach, and dropped to his knees.

Candy's concern soon turned to fear as she watched her beloved doctor change into something she could barely describe.

As her owner heaved himself upright, his shoulders spread...

His neck thickened and his hands turned into giant, hairy claws...

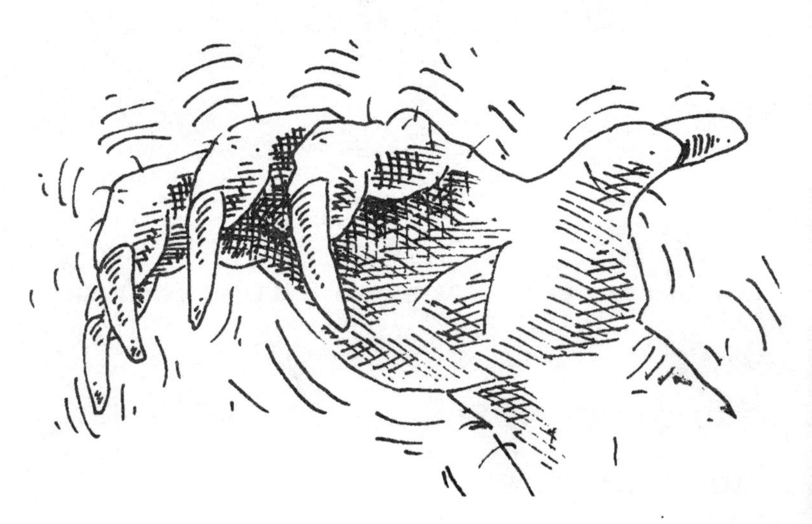

Veins stood out on his skin. His hair grew long and wiry.

His yellow, bloodshot eyes opened and met Candy's terrified stare.

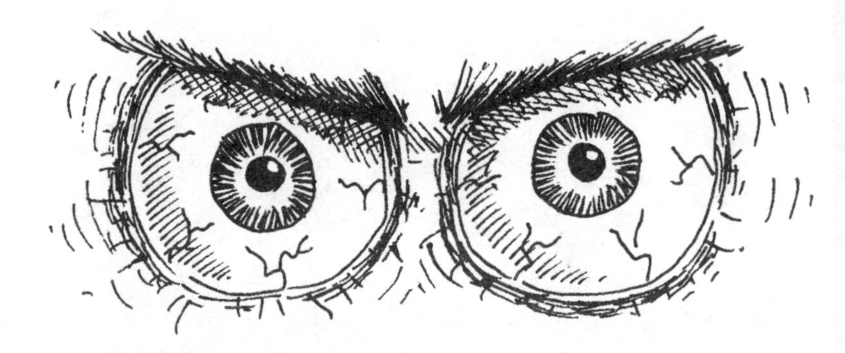

A wicked grin spread across his cracked and twisted mouth.

"At last! I'm free of that oh so terribly nicey-nice doctor," he hissed.

The creature moved towards Candy.

She backed away from him in fear. His eyes were wild as he whispered to her. Spit dribbled down his chin.

"All my life I've been hidden inside that silly little doctor. I made him make that medicine to release me. It's goodbye Doctor Catkyll – hello Mr Hyde!"

Suddenly, Candy made a dash for the catflap. Quick as a flash she was outside. Mr Hyde let out a low howl of rage and followed her into the night.

HOWWLL!

Candy would have left any normal human behind, but Mr Hyde had animal speed. Her heart pounded as she raced into the darkness.

Mr Hyde had gained other animal traits too. He could see in the dark and follow the scent of Candy's trail.

Candy heard Mr Hyde chasing her...

...crashing through bushes...

...tossing dustbins aside...

...smashing his way through fences. Nothing could stop him.

At the railway line, Candy raced along the tracks until they disappeared into a tunnel. She was too frightened to go in.

On either side, the banks were too steep for her to climb. She could hear Mr Hyde's rasping, heavy breath close behind.

The dark, gaping mouth of the tunnel offered no comfort.

Did a light move in the distance? What was that quivering sound she could hear? Candy froze, not knowing what to do, or which way to turn.

In that moment of hesitation, Mr Hyde appeared behind her and scooped her up into his huge, hairy hands.

"Gotcha!" he sneered.

Candy felt his foul breath on her face. A cruel smile played at the corner of his mouth. His hands circled round Candy's neck. She couldn't breathe!

She fought for breath...

...Mr Hyde's grip tightened.

She felt herself slipping away. She looked at her tormenter and pleaded with her eyes.

For a moment, Mr Hyde faded away and the good Doctor Catkyll returned.

He let go of Candy and stared at his hands in horror. “How could I destroy what I love so much?” he gasped.

Candy saw the light in the tunnel grow stronger and heard the swishing of the rails get louder. She hauled her battered body to the side of the tracks.

The good doctor was turning back into his terrifying other self. "I can never return," Doctor Catkyll called. "I must destroy Mr Hyde before he destroys us all!"

A dazzling light made Doctor Catkyll's figure a silhouette in the mouth of the tunnel.

Its shape changed back and forth.

One moment, Candy could see her kind doctor.

Next she saw the hideous shape of Mr Hyde! It was like watching two people fighting for their lives.

A deafening sound filled the air. It drowned the screams as the good doctor forced Mr Hyde onto the tracks. Mr Hyde fell into the path of the train that burst out of the tunnel, horns blaring, headlights ablaze!

BLAAH!

The secret circle held their breath. From far away, Molly heard her own doctor call. “Molly! Come home now!”

"I'd better go," said Molly nervously.

"You watch that good doctor of yours," said Kipling. "Make sure she doesn't get a taste for her own medicine!"

Shoo Rayner

❑ Frankatstein	1 84362 729 9	£3.99
❑ Foggy Moggy Inn	1 84362 730 2	£3.99
❑ Catula	1 84362 731 0	£3.99
❑ Catkin Farm	1 84362 732 9	£3.99
❑ Bluebeard's Cat	1 84362 733 7	£3.99
❑ The Killer Catflap	1 84362 744 2	£3.99
❑ Dr Catkyll and Mr Hyde	1 84362 745 0	£3.99
❑ Catnapped	1 84362 746 9	£3.99

Little HORRORS

❑ The Swamp Man	1 84121 646 1	£3.99
❑ The Pumpkin Man	1 84121 644 5	£3.99
❑ The Spider Man	1 84121 648 8	£3.99
❑ The Sand Man	1 84121 650 X	£3.99
❑ The Shadow Man	1 84362 021 X	£3.99
❑ The Bone Man	1 84362 010 3	£3.99
❑ The Snow Man	1 84362 009 X	£3.99
❑ The Bogey Man	1 84362 011 1	£3.99

These books are available from all good bookshops,
or can be ordered direct from the publisher:
Orchard Books, PO BOX 29, Douglas IM99 1BQ
Credit card orders please telephone 01624 836000 or fax 01624 837033
or e-mail: bookshop@enterprise.net for details.

To order please quote title, author and ISBN and your full name and address.
Cheques and postal orders should be made payable to 'Bookpost plc'.
Postage and packing is FREE within the UK
(overseas customers should add £1.00 per book).

Prices and availability are subject to change.